It was a dark and stormy night ...

Just the sort of night, in fact, to curl up on the sofa and watch my favourite horror video, *I Was Frankenstein's Monster's Vampire Werewolf*. So I did just that.

Then I thought it might be more exciting if instead of just *watching* the video, I actually put it in the VCR and switched on the telly.

So I did. But the picture that appeared before me on the screen wasn't of Frankenstein's vampire werewolf. It was a picture of a sheep.

My big sister came in and peered over my shoulder with her great big beady eyes. "What *are* you watching?" she asked.

"*I Was Frankenstein's Monster's Vampire Werewolf,*" I replied.

"That's not a werewolf," she said, looking at the sheep on the screen. Dead sharp my big sister is.

"No," I replied, "you're right. Perhaps it's a werewool."

"A were*wool?*"

"Yes, a sheep that thinks it's a werewolf."

"Phoo-ey," said my big sister, "it's our kid's *Learn To Count With Postman Pat* video!"

And suddenly I realized she was right! My little four-year-old brother had swapped his *Learn to Count With Postman Pat* video for my vampire werewolf one and was no doubt watching it on the other telly in the back room! What a Joker!

I was well fed up (I'd had two Double Whoppaburgers and Extra Fries for tea, you see). I was also well cheesed off, angry and furious. Not to mention livid. But it's too late now. I have. Mentioned livid, that is.

I knew what I had to do. Not only I, but people across the world – yes, people like you – had to be rescued from the clutches of their Joker brothers. There is, of course, only one person capable of succeeding in such a mission.

"Who? *Who?*" I hear you ask. (Yes, amazing hearing I've got.)

"Is it a pain?" you think.

A pain? No, that's your big brother.

"Is it a bird?"

A bird? No, that's your big brother's girlfriend.

It's me! BRATMAN! And, of course, my faithful old nag, Dobbin.

Yes, Dobbin and I would help all decent law-abiding people learn how to handle their brothers.

But first of all I was going to get that video back. It took me an hour and a half. And this was only possible because I used some advice I'd got from a very useful book called *101 Handy Tips From The Spanish Inquisition*.

However, when I got back to the front room, I found the telly had disappeared! But that's another story[1].

1: Which you can read on page 1 of *How To Handle Your Sister*. To do this, follow these instructions: either stay sitting where you are, turn to the back of this book then turn it the other way up, or turn to the back of this book, keep it the same way up and stand on your head.

Two hours later I was on the streets on Coffsweet City. A few days later the threat from those Joker-brats, a.k.a. brothers, was no more and I was the toast of the town.

This was unfortunate, as I have a particular aversion to being shoved under a blazing hot grill and then having butter and marmalade smeared all over me.

If you want to know the secrets of my success in handling brothers, then all you have to do is read on ...

ON

Right. Now you're right **on**, why not turn over and read the rest of the book?

Scholastic Children's Books,
Commonwealth House, 1-19 New Oxford Street,
London WC1A 1NU, UK
a division of Scholastic Ltd
London ~ New York ~ Toronto ~ Sydney ~ Auckland

Published in the UK by Scholastic Ltd, 1998

Text copyright © Roy Apps, 1998
Illustrations copyright © Nick Sharratt, 1998

ISBN 0 590 19684 7

All rights reserved

Typeset by Rapid Reprographics
Printed by Cox & Wyman Ltd, Reading, Berks.

All rights reserved

10 9 8 7 6 5 4 3 2 1

The right of Roy Apps and Nick Sharratt to be identified as the author and illustrator of this work respectively has been asserted by them in accordance with the Copyright, Designs and Patents Act, 1988.

This book is sold subject to the condition that it shall not, by way of trade or otherwise, be lent, resold, hired out, or otherwise circulated without the publisher's prior consent in any form of binding other than that in which it is published and without a similar condition, including this condition, being imposed upon the subsequent purchaser.

How To Handle Your Brother

By Roy Apps

Illustrated by Nick Sharratt

Contents

How To Handle Your Brother: Stage One

Just like the Joker, brothers[1] have the power to take on various disguises. These are likely to be related to their favourite films and telly shows. But don't worry! Once you've read Bratman's Guide to Your Brother's Disguises, everything will be just like a really boring English lesson. In other words,

All Write!

Bratman: I suppose you mean "ALL RIGHT." If only you'd paid attention during lessons instead of sitting in the back going "dinnadinnadinnadinna" all the time, you might have learnt some English!

E R E Gore-Blimey (your old English teacher at Coffsweet City Juniors)

1: And for that matter, sisters (see *How To Handle Your Sister* page 10).

BRATMAN AND DOBBIN'S GUIDE TO YOUR BROTHER'S DISGUISES

Brother Disguise 1: **Junior Master Chef**

The first person I ran into on the streets of Coffsweet City was in a terrified state. Hardly surprising, as I'd just run into him.

He told me his name was Paul. "Not Paul Thechain?" I asked. He nodded. "You've gone bright red," I said. "Oh, I'm often flushed," he replied.

Paul went on to tell me about the terrible problems he was having with his brother: "It all started one day when my mum said, 'Your brother's really keen on this Junior Master Chef thing, isn't he?'"

"And is he?" I asked. Paul shook his head.

"Of course, he's not," I went on. "Because Junior Master Chef is only his Joker-type disguise. There's only one method of cooking up what he's interested in, and it's not frying it, grilling it, baking it, mixing it or boiling it – it's *stirring it*. Real Junior Master Chefs are, of course, inoffensive little chaps who say things like:

"Your brother in his Junior Master Chef disguise on the other hand, not to mention the other leg, says things like..."

"Mum, Paul's putting chilli powder in the pepper mill!" said Paul.

"Exactly. In other words, whereas a real Junior Master Chef likes nothing more than to fill a pudding bowl with flour and then to stir it, your brother in his Junior Master Chef disguise likes nothing more than to fill your mum's head with a lot of tales about your harmless little practical jokes and then to stir it."

Genuine
Junior Master Chef

Joker
Junior Master Chef

"And just like a Junior Master Chef contestant with a plate of prawn balls and a deep fat fryer, your brother in a Junior Master Chef disguise will relish any opportunity he can get to drop you in it."

"I'd really like to become a real Junior Master Chef, so that I could boil my brother's big head in a sizzling hot saucepan, or beat him thoroughly with an egg whisk."

"That's just the sort of thing a caring and sensitive brother like yourself would like to do," I said. "But it is not a good idea. It will only result in unnecessary pain and suffering as your mum tells you off for burning the bottom of her best saucepan, or bending her best egg whisk."

"So, can I learn to handle him?" asked Paul, with an anxious look.

"Of course!" I assured him.

Handling Your Brother's Junior Master Chef Disguise:

Dobbin and I offer you this advice:

"Alternatively, look at it this way. There are only two things to do with a Junior Master Chef Joker. Either you can egg on him. By that, I mean crack half a dozen eggs over his head. Then the *yolk's* on him. Add a packet of millet, then it'll be a really corny yolk.

"For the best results though, don't egg on him, but egg him on."

I explained to Paul how this would work and we went to his house to try it out. This is what happened:

Shhh! Don't tell Mum, but I'm going to put chilli powder in the pepper mill!

PAUL'S BROTHER: Mum! Paul's put chilli powder in the pepper mill!

PAUL'S MUM: (*Looks in the pepper mill)* I can't see any chilli powder in here...(*to Paul's brother*) you're not telling fibs just to try and get your brother into trouble are you?

She chases Paul's brother out of the room.

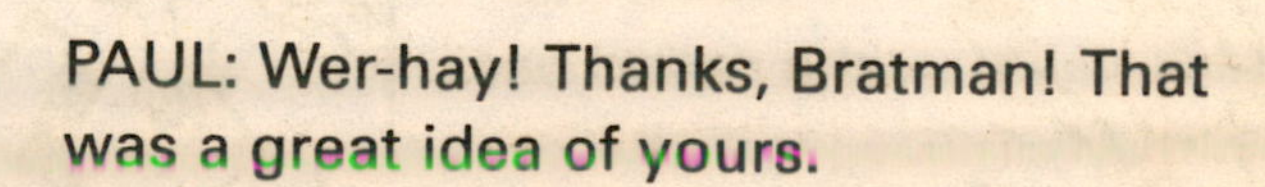

PAUL: Wer-hay! Thanks, Bratman! That was a great idea of yours.

I smiled modestly.

PAUL: Even better was your idea to put pepper in the tissue box, Bratman!

I smiled modestly, again.

Unfortunately, Paul was laughing so much, that tears started to run down his face. Keen to wipe them away before they ran out of breath, he took a paper hanky from the tissue box...

Brother Disguise 2: **The O-Men**

After Dobbin and I left Paul Thechain's house, we rode off along the dark streets of Coffsweet City. As we passed, a young girl jumped out of the way.

"Just in time!" I shouted.

"That's me," she called back.

"Eh?"

"That's my name. Jess Tintime."

I'd rather guessed it would be. Jess invited Dobbin and me back to her place for a can of Coke. We were sitting in the kitchen when, suddenly, a furious figure burst into the room. He was livid. So I said, "Hi, Livid!"

This was a mistake, because this hideous creature hadn't got my sense of humour. In fact, it hadn't got anybody's sense of humour, not even its own.

It was a strange beast. It looked like a table lamp: in other words, it appeared to be alight. At least, its hair was bright red. Not only that, but its eyes were looming, its ears were fuming and its voice was booming.

"Ooooooohhhh!" it boomed. "Ooooooohhhh!"

And, immediately, I knew what it was. "Jess," I yelled, "it's one of the crazy half-man, half-beast monsters from the film about a group of aliens possessed by the devil who can only say 'Oh!', *The O-Men*!"

"What shall we do?" trembled Jess.

"No probs!" I said. "I know, from having seen the film at the Coffsweet City Multiscreen, that all you need to do to handle one of the O-Men is to give them a blast with an Intergalactic Extra-Terrestrial Super-Charged Laser Ray Gun!"

I was about to go out and look to see if Dobbin had a spare one of these in his saddlebag, when the O-Man pointed to his hair and said: "You blathering great hooligan!"

This came as a bit of a surprise. Mainly, because O-Men are only meant to be able to say "Oh".

Then Jess said, "It isn't one of the O-Men, it's my big brother!"

Yes, Jess was right. It *was* her big brother disguised in a Joker-type disguise as one of the O-Men! Why should he do such a thing? He was still pointing to his hair and blabbing on. I could pick out only a few words, such as "natural", "born" and "killer".

Then I picked out a few more words – addressed to Jess.
The words were:

"You moronic nincompoop! What did you want to fill the wash 'n' go bottle up with tomato ketchup for?"

To which Jess replied, "Because I couldn't find the Thousand Island Dressing."

This was a bit of a mistake on Jess's part, because – strange as it may seem – Jess's brother couldn't see the joke. This, of course, might have been because his eyes were full of dollops of ketchup.

"Bratman! Dobbin! What shall I do?" pleaded Jess.

Handling Your Brother's O-Men Disguise:

"Jess," I said, "the only thing to do with a brother like yours, who has disguised himself as one of the O-Men, is to exorcise the demon. He is, after all, like a man possessed. You could use a cross, but this is unlikely to work as your brother seems to have got cross already. You could try the old stake through the heart routine, but the price of meat these days means you'd be lucky to be able to afford a bag of tripe, let alone an old stake. No, the best way of warding off your brother is to use garlic."

Bratman: Steak, as in meat is spelt s.t.e.a.k. not s.t.a.k.e. If you were still at school I'd ask you to see me at brake!

E R E Gore-Blimey (your old English teacher)

1: Dobbin, of course, is terrified by day horses. On the other hand, he isn't at all frightened by *night mares*. In fact, he's rather fond of them.

Now, in the films, all they have to do is to hold the garlic up in front of the demon's face. But seeing how mad Jess's brother was, I decided it would be better for her to chew a couple of cloves. So she did.

When her brother approached her saying, "Ooooooohhhh!!" I yelled, "Breathe out, Jess!"

And she did. Long and slow.

Jubilation! Jess's brother immediately stopped snarling and going "Ooooooohhhh!!" and started holding his nose and going "Pooooohhhh!!"

In a few seconds he was out of the house and halfway down the road trying to get away from the smell of garlic.

Brother Disguise 3: **Red Dwarf**

In a few more seconds, Dobbin and I were out of Jess Tintime's house and halfway down the road trying to get away from the smell of garlic, too. We pulled up outside the front gate of a small house. Suddenly, a girl came running out.

"Quick! Hide!" she said. "And cover your ears!"

We crouched down behind the fence. Dobbin and I introduced ourselves.

"My name's Ali," said the girl. "Ali Gator."

Then without warning, a dreadful scream filled the air.

I peered over the fence. In the doorway I saw something small and loud and red. It had a face like a squashed tomato. I had no doubt what it was: Ali's little brother in his Joker-type Red Dwarf disguise.

Out came Ali's mum.

"Grrrr!" she said.

She had obviously seen red. Not surprising really, given that she was staring at Ali's little brother.

She caught Ali peeping over the fence. "What's going on here, Ali?"

"Wahhh blah sniff burble boooo!" said Red Dwarf.

"I thought you were old enough to know better!"

This is a typical result of having a little brother who uses a Red Dwarf disguise.

Even though she hasn't the slightest idea what Red Dwarf's on about, Ali's mum just assumes it's all her fault! Yes, even though it's Red Dwarf who's making a racket, Ali's the one who's in trouble!

"What happened?" I asked Ali.

Ali explained it all. "I was sitting in the kitchen, spraying my hair with Mum's blue shoe polish to try and give myself a well smart 'bad girl' look, when he came in wanting to know where Freddy the Teddy was."

"And what did you tell him?"

"Just a harmless little tale ... along the lines of 'Oh, I don't know. I expect he's been kidnapped by a gang of ruthless aliens, taken off to the dark side of the Planet Glurg and been boiled alive in a volcanic crater.'"

I shook my head sympathetically.

"Then his fists started turning a funny colour..."

"Red?" I asked.

"No, blue."

"Blue?"

"Yes, I realized I was accidentally spraying him with the blue shoe polish." Ali sighed. "I've got to do something about my little brother."

"Yes, indeed," I agreed.

"I suppose I could treat the tomato-faced little bawler just like you'd treat any other tomato. That is, stuff it. Say ... a couple of cucumbers in his ears, a cos lettuce in his mouth and a radish up each nostril... What do you think, Bratman?"

"Of course, it is a very tempting course of action, particularly for a caring and sensitive brother or sister like yourself. There is a drawback, though. For although doing this will certainly shut him up, it'll mean you're short of garnish to put in your burger at teatime."

"Oh dear! What do you suggest, then, Bratman?"

Handling Your Brother's Red Dwarf Disguise:

"It's a difficult problem, this."

"It's a difficult little brother, this," replied Ali. "What do you say, Dobbin?"

If your brother carries on like that he'll soon become a Shetland pony[1]!

"I'm afraid there is nothing you can do to make your brother stop that awful racket," I said.

Ali looked glum.

1: i.e. a little ho(a)rse.

"But," I went on, "you can make some dosh out of him. What you do is hire him out as an auxiliary fire engine. The racket he makes sounds just like a wailing siren and the buckets of water he's producing from all the crying is enough to put out any fire."

"Thanks, Bratman," said Ali.

"Neee-ahhh! Neee-ahhh!" wailed Ali's little brother as they set off for the nearest fire.

Brother Disguise 4: **Robbing Hood**

On through the streets of Coffsweet City trotted Dobbin and I. A boy hailed us from his front drive.

"Bratman! You must help me!"

Dobbin and I went over to him.

"My name's Ravi," he said.

"Let me guess," I replied. "Ravi Oli?"

Ravi nodded.

"What's your problem?" I asked him.

"It's my brother—" he began.

At that moment, a brand-new, thirty-seven gear, turquoise and purple mountain bike with an alloy frame whizzed past us, just brushing our noses. It was being ridden by a little chap dressed all in Lincoln green with a bow and a quiver of arrows slung across his back.

The first thing Ravi said was: "What's my brand-new, thirty-seven gear, turquoise and purple mountain bike with an alloy frame doing with a brush?"

The second thing Ravi said was: "Come back with my bike, you little vandal!"

The third thing Ravi said was: "I'll ******[1] your ******[1] to the *****[1], you wait!!!"

The fourth thing Ravi said was: "I hope the Sheriff of Nottingham catches you and flings you into a rat-infested dungeon."

The fifth thing Ravi said was: "Hey no! He'd better not. My bike'll get scratched!"

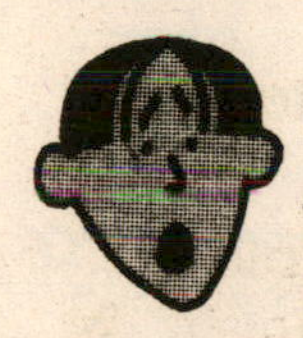

The sixth thing Ravi said was: "That's not Robin Hood, it can't be, there aren't any Merry Men with him!"[2]

The first thing *I* said was: "You're right, that's not Robin Hood, that's your Joker-like brother in his latest disguise – Robbing Hood!"[3]

"Come back with my bike!" yelled Ravi.

"I'm only borrowing it!" his brother called out over his shoulder.

1: Words too rude to even print.

2: This is true. In fact, the only other person about is *you* and merry is definitely not how *you* feel.

3: For a note on the female version of this disguise – Sister Hood – see *How To Handle Your Sister*, page 27.

This, of course, was a lot of phoo-ey. *Borrowers*, as those of you who have read the books or seen the TV programmes know, are meek little people who live under the floorboards. Which brothers certainly don't. More's the pity.

"You know what I'm going to do to him, don't you?" said Ravi.

"Yes," I replied. "You've already told me.[1] But that's going to make a very nasty mess on the pavement, isn't it? It won't do your dad's garden fork much good, either."

"So, what do you suggest?" asked Ravi.

1: See Ravi's third thought on page 29.

Handling Your Brother's Robbing Hood Disguise:

"The best thing to do with a brother using the Robbing Hood disguise is to give your bike the old Happy Days Colouring Book treatment. That is, fill it in."

Colouring book

Mountain bike

So, next day, Ravi and I stuffed the alloy frame of his bike with the heaviest things we could find, which was three of his gran's sponge puddings and a rolled-up copy of his dad's Sunday paper.

Then we waited for his little brother to don his Joker-type Robbing Hood disguise.

Out he came, climbed on to Ravi's bike, then...

"Aaaargh!" he yelled, as he fell off under the weight.
Then, "Aaaargh!" he yelled again as he fell off under the bike.
Leaving Ravi's bike on top of him.

And leaving Ravi on top of the world!

Brother Disguise 5: **Gladiator**

On and on I rode, through the streets of Coffsweet City. Sitting on the pavement outside a large house, I espied a young girl.

"Hi!" I called.
"I can see you're really upset."
"Yes," she sniffed. "That's me. Ria Lee-Upset. It's my brother."

"Isn't it always?" Dobbin sighed.[1]

"My brother and me were—"

"And I," I corrected her.

"Were you there, too, Bratman?" asked Ria.

"No ... I was correcting your grammar," I explained.

That's my job, Bratman!
Stick to what you're good at
i.e. dealing with Joker-type brothers.
E R E Gore-Blimey (your old English teacher)

"I'm always getting things wrong," said Ria. "Anyway, me and me brother was watching this video, *Revenge of the Killer Hamsters*." He was wearing his Lycra leotard.

1: No!!!! Is the answer to this one. And if you don't believe me, try reading *How To Handle Your Sister*!

"At the end of the film, Sally Wagg, the girl who's been trying to save the world from the Killer Hamsters gets killed and eaten by the evil King Hamster. I was very upset."

"I don't suppose Sally was too happy about it, either," I said.

Ria ignored my comment. "My brother thought it was funny. He said, 'I'm glad he ate her!'"

"And do you know why he said that?" I asked Ria.

She shook her head.

"Your brother was in his Joker-type Gladiator disguise! That's why he said 'I'm Glad-he-ate-her!'"

"What shall I do, Bratman?" sighed Ria.

Handling Your Brother's Gladiator Disguise:

"Leave this to me!" I said.

Quickly, I took the rat's tail, nuts and witch's whiskers from my Bratman Out-To-Lunch Box.[1] I stuck the tail on Dobbin's bottom and the whiskers on his face. Then I told him to get eating the nuts.

When Ria's brother came out, he took one look at Dobbin and yelled: "Aaaargh!!!! It's a Killer Hamster!"

And he tore up the road.[2]

1: See *How To Handle Your Sister* page 39.

2: The council workmen came and laid it back, later.

"Thanks, Bratman!" beamed Ria. "And thank you, Dobbin!"

If you need to handle your brother's Gladiator disguise, and you haven't got a horse like Dobbin, use somebody who looks like a horse. Your big brother's girlfriend, say.

The most famous brothers of all, who wore Joker-type Gladiator disguises, spent all their time making up really grim and gruesome stories. They were known as the Brothers Grim.

TEST YOURSELF!!!! On Brothers' Joker-type Disguises

1 Which of the following television programmes are also Joker-type disguises used by brothers:

(i) Red Dwarf
(ii) Blue Peter
(iii) Pink Panther

2 What is ******!:

(i) Something unpronounceable
(ii) Something unmentionable
(iii) Something unprintable

3 While undertaking scientific experiments into flight, using paper aeroplanes, you realize that the paper you've been using is (or rather was) your brother's GCSE History project. What disguise is he likely to use when he finds out?

(i) The Mister Men
(ii) The O-Men
(iii) The O Zone

HOW TO SCORE:

1: (i) Take 3 points. Then quickly give them to your little brother before he puts on a Joker-type Red Dwarf disguise and starts screaming the place down.

(ii) Take 1 point. Not strictly a Joker-type disguise, but you will probably argue that Blue Peter is a good description of Ali Gator's brother after she attacked him with the boot polish while she was trying to perfect that "bad girl" look (see page 24). OK. Fair enough. I take your point. Which leaves you with 0 points. Hee-hee!

(iii) Take half a point. Pink Panther is what little sisters tend to call their twinkie trikes.

2: **(i)** Take ****** points.

(ii) If it's unmentionable you shouldn't have mentioned it, should you? No points.

(iii) How can it be? I've just printed it – if you take my point. Go on, then. Take it.

3: **(i)** No points. Though seeing what kind of mood your brother's in, it would probably be a good idea if you Missed, er, this particular Man for the next few weeks.

(ii) Take 3 points. Don't let your brother get them, though, or else he'll probably start sticking them into a wax effigy of you.

(iii) No points. The O Zone is the twelve kilometre Out Of Bounds zone around your brother, until he calms down (i.e. next Easter).

How To Handle Your Brother: Stage Two

BRATMAN AND DOBBIN'S GUIDE TO ESSENTIAL BROTHER-HANDLING EQUIPMENT

The following items of equipment are essential for successful brother-handling:

1: The Bratman Mask

See opposite.

This will enable you to go about your brother-handling missions undetected. All you need to do is to cut it out, then cut out holes for the string and your eyes. Then thread the string through them. The holes that is, not your eyes.

However, if you don't want to cut holes for the eyes, just put it over your face – it will save you having to look at your brother when he uses his O-Men disguise.

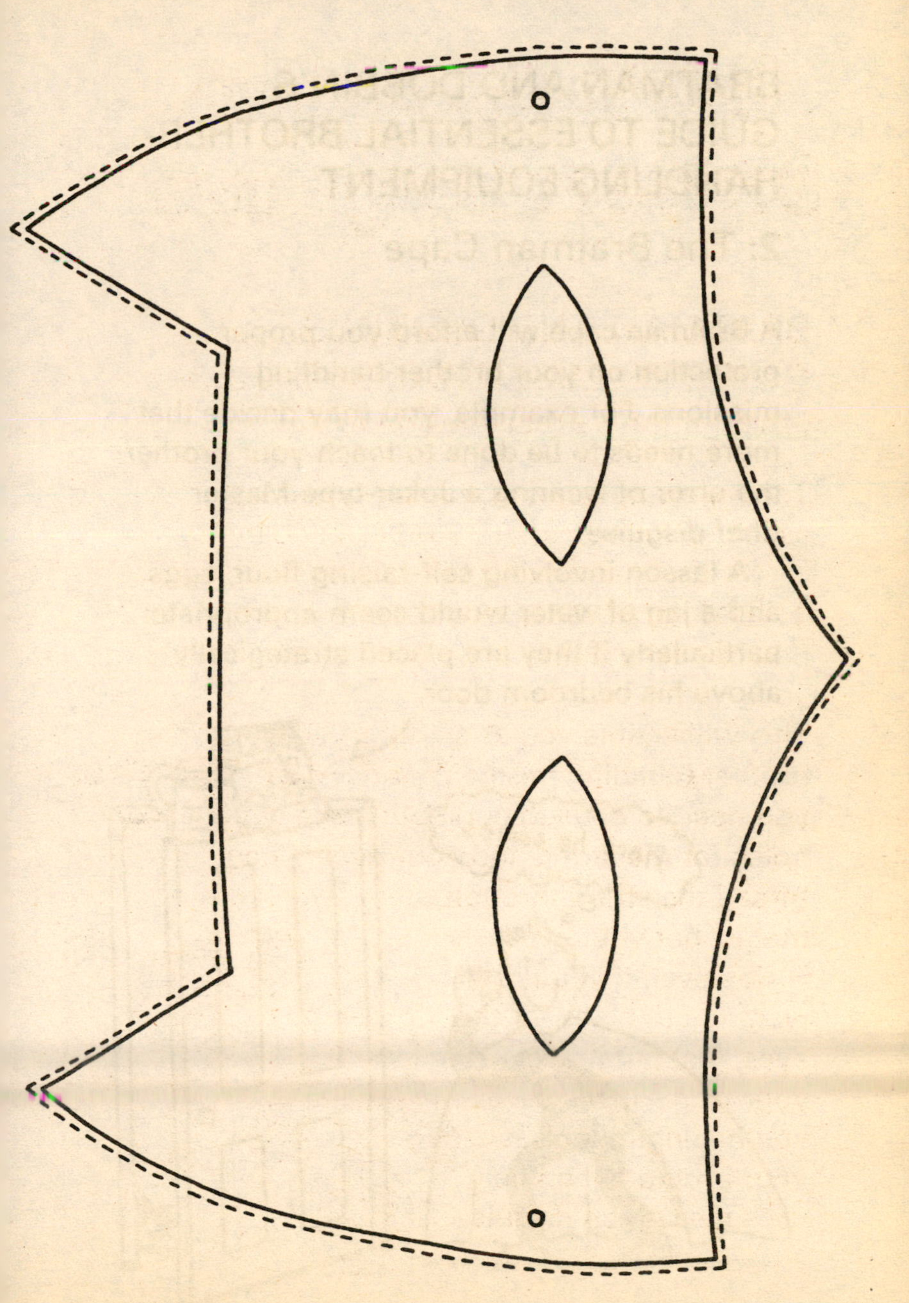

BRATMAN AND DOBBIN'S GUIDE TO ESSENTIAL BROTHER-HANDLING EQUIPMENT

2: The Bratman Cape

A Bratman cape will afford you proper protection on your brother-handling missions. For example, you may decide that more needs to be done to teach your brother the error of wearing a Joker-type Master Chef disguise.

A lesson involving self-raising flour, eggs and a jug of water would seem appropriate: particularly if they are placed strategically above his bedroom door.

The danger, of course, is that when your brother pushes the door open, you might inadvertently cop some of the deluge. However, a Bratman Cape will ensure that you are well covered.

BRATMAN AND DOBBIN'S GUIDE TO ESSENTIAL BROTHER-HANDLING EQUIPMENT

3: Bratman Pie-jamas

Bratman Pie-jamas are just the thing to wear at night on your brother-handling missions. Bratman Pie-jamas are made of cheese and onion pies, fruit pies and custard pies. The really well-smart thing about Bratman Pie-jamas is that however long you may have to wait – for example, before catching your brother sneaking out in his Robbing Hood disguise to have a go on your skateboard – you will never go hungry!

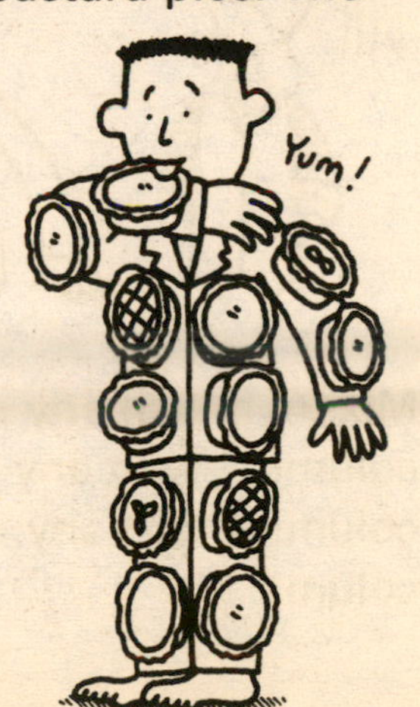

How To Handle Your Brother: Stage Three

BRATMAN AND DOBBIN'S FIVE CHART TOPPING INSULTS TO HURL AT BROTHERS

Astound and annoy your brother by using Bratman and Dobbin's unique range of very rude-sounding insults.

Mix 'n' match any one insulting word from column 1 with any insulting word from column 2 and any insulting word from column 3.

1	2	3
goongilly	plop	nurdler
pathetic	gunge	bumbler
fickedded	blob	boggler
excruciating	futtock	dribbler
nin	com	poop

Practise here:

"You're a
.........1......... ....2.........
with the brains of a
.........2......... ....3........."

"You're a
.........1......... ....2.........
with the sense of a ....2.........
.........3......... ....3........."

"You're a
.........1......... ....2.........
with the manners of a ....2.........
.........3........."

How To Handle Your Brother: Stage Four

CHECKLIST!!!!!

Check which Joker-type disguises your brother uses:

1 Does your brother ever say:

(i) "Mum, you'll never guess what our Kevin's doing – he's cleaning his bike in the bath!"
(ii) "Mum, you'll never guess what our Kevin's doing – All Day Breakfasts!"
(iii) "Mum, you'll never guess what our Kevin's blurgleblurgleblurgle!!!"

2 Does your brother ever say:

(i) "Oooooooo!!!!"
(ii) "Just wait until I ketchup with you!"
(iii) "Grrr! Grrr!"

3 Has your brother got a face like:

(i) a squashed tomato
(ii) a turnip
(iii) a mangoldwurzel

4 Does your brother wear:

(i) *your* best bomber jacket
(ii) a suit of Lincoln green
(iii) a two-centimetre
covering of custard and cream

5 Does your brother ever wear:

(i) a leotard
(ii) a leopard
(iii) a large sheet of white metal

ANSWERS:

1: **(i)** Call Bratman and Dobbin immediately! Your brother's using a Junior Master Chef disguise.

(ii) Don't panic! Your brother's using a Little Chef disguise.

(iii) No probs! Your brother's using a ROBO CHEF disguise.

2: **(i)** Call Bratman and Dobbin immediately! Your brother's using an O-MEN disguise!

(ii) Don't panic! Your brother's using a HEE-HEE-MEN disguise. He's pun-ny like that. (Chances are he's puny like that, too.)

(iii) No probs! Your brother's one of the HE-MEN. So watch out.

3: **(i)** Call Bratman and Dobbin immediately! Your brother's using a RED DWARF disguise.

(ii) You must be confusing him with your sister.

(iii) How do you know? Have you ever seen a mangoldwurzel? Do you even know what a mangoldwurzel is?[1]

1: Well, let me tell you: it's a large kind of root vegetable, a bit like a turnip, used mainly for feeding cows. (*The Bratman & Dobbin Dictionary*)

4: (i) Call Bratman and Dobbin immediately! Your brother's using a Robbing Hood disguise.

(ii) Don't panic! Your brother's the famous outlaw ROBIN HOOD. He's also got the dress sense of a mixed salad.

(iii) No probs! Your brother's the famous speciality dessert, ROBIN PUD.

5: (i) Call Bratman and Dobbin immediately! Your brother's using a GLADIATOR disguise.

(ii) Don't panic! Your brother's decided on a career working with wild animals. (Quite sensible really, seeing as he resembles one himself.)

(iii) No probs! Your brother's disguised himself as a RADIATOR.

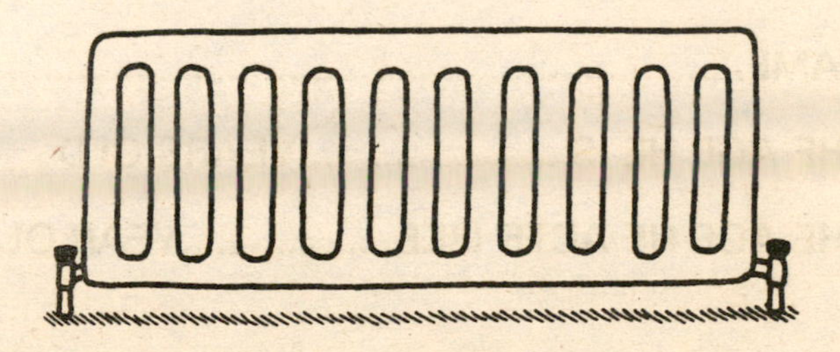

How To Handle Your Brother : Stage Five

THE BRATMAN AND DOBBIN BROTHER'S JOKER-TYPE DISGUISE FILE

Draw your brother below.

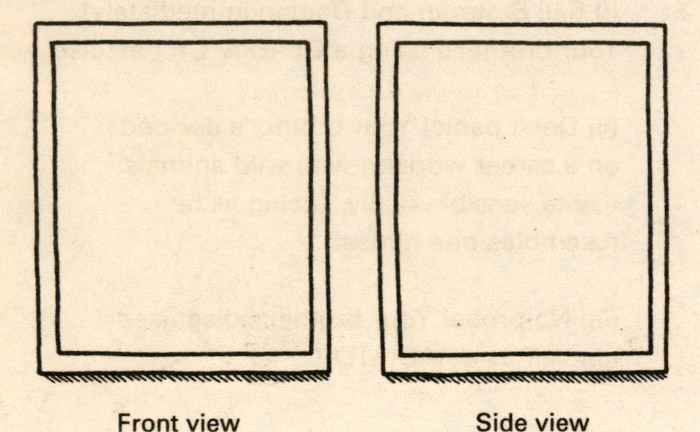

Front view

Side view

NAME...

THE AGE HE IS:.......................YEARS OLD

THE AGE HE ACTS LIKE..................YEAR OLD

HIS JOKER-TYPE DISGUISES

(tick relevant box)

1 DOES HE USE THE
MASTER CHEF DISGUISE?

YES ☐
NO ☐

IF YES, DOES HIS MASTER CHEF DISGUISE MAKE HIM LOOK LIKE:

(i) A great dollop of lard? ☐
(ii) A great dollop of pudding? ☐
(iii) A great dollop? ☐

2 DOES HE USE THE
O-MEN DISGUISE?

YES ☐
NO ☐

IF YES, DOES HIS O-MEN DISGUISE MAKE HIM LOOK:

(i) Scarifying? ☐
(ii) Terrifying? ☐
(iii) Lairy-fying? ☐

3 DOES HE USE A
RED DWARF DISGUISE?

YES ☐
NO ☐

IF YES, DOES HIS RED DWARF DISGUISE MAKE HIM LOOK:

(i) All hot and sweaty? ☐
(ii) All hop and sweaty? ☐

(iii) All hip and swotty? ☐

4 DOES HE USE THE **ROBBING HOOD** DISGUISE?

YES ☐
NO ☐

IF YES, DOES HE DO HIS ROBBING WITH:

(i) His right hand; making him a right little nicker? ☐
(ii) His left hand; making him a left little nicker? ☐
(iii) With his mate; making them both a pair of knickers? ☐

5 DOES HE USE THE **GLADIATOR** DISGUISE?

YES ☐
NO ☐

IF YES, DOES HIS GLADIATOR DISGUISE MAKE HIM LOOK LIKE A:

(i) Wolf ☐
(ii) Werewolf [1] ☐
(iii) Werewool [1] ☐

Baa!

1: See page 2.

How To Handle Your Brother : Stage Six

THE BRATMAN AND DOBBIN PRETTY GOOD USES FOR A BROTHER FILE

1 THINGS HE CAN GANG UP WITH ME ON AGAINST DAD
(e.g. definitions of "a tidy room"; buying that Irish Wolfhound puppy; only having to visit your Auntie Ermintrude once every four years and not once every four weeks.)

1...
....
....

2...
....
....

3...
....
....

4...
....
....

5...
....
....

2 INFORMATION I CAN GET FROM HIM
(e.g. about the secret life of Mr Jekyll [Head of Year 9]; about what happens behind the school kitchens; about how Uncle Cecil got his false leg.)

1...
....
....

2...
....
....

3...
....
....

4...
....
....

5...
....
....

3 BRIBES I CAN USE ON HIM
(e.g. if you don't let me borrow your bike, I'll tell Mum who let the dog eat her spinach and lentil loaf.)

1...
....
....

2...
....
....

3...
....
....

4...
....
....

5...
....
....